Wally's
Misadventure

To
Ravi
&
Prubby

ADemer

:)

ISBN 978-1-63575-849-8 (paperback)
ISBN 978-1-63575-850-4 (digital)

Christian Faith Publishing, Inc.
832 Park Avenue
Meadville, PA 16335
www.christianfaithpublishing.com

Printed in the United States of America

Wally's Misadventure

Chrys Wimer

Wally Raccoon had been begging his parents to let him go on an adventure with his friends for weeks, but between his lessons and chores, he never had time. Today, Wally got up early and was able to finish his to-do list before breakfast.

"I've finished my chores early! Can I go play with my friends now? Please, pleeeeeeease?" he asked his father.

"Of course you may go, but remember the rules," said his father.

"Yes, Dad," said Wally over his shoulder as he ran toward the pond.

Looking around, Wally saw Aspen Beaver near the edge of the pond carefully gnawing off every branch of a newly fallen tree.

"Howdy, Aspen!" yelled Wally.

Aspen didn't look up, but she greeted Wally with a flip of her tail. Wally walked closer and sat down to watch. When she finished, Aspen looked up with a big beaver grin.

"Howdy to you too, W-W-Wally. W-w-w-what's happ-p-pening?" Aspen said.

"I want to go on an adventure, and I was wondering if you would like to join me?"

"Gnawwww, I'm t-tooo b-b-busy. My dad is going to teach me how to fix the b-b-breach in the dam. Can't have a leak, you know."

Aspen went back to work on her log, so Wally shrugged his shoulders and walked away.

Next, he found Ivy Wren sitting in her favorite tree singing a song he had never heard before. Wally listened for a while before interrupting.

"Good morning, Ivy," said Wally.

"Oh, how are you this lovely day? Did you come for a singing lesson?" Ivy asked.

"No, I was wondering if you would like to go on an adventure with me."

"I'm so sorry, my dear. I have been working on this song for days, and I can't seem to get the ending right. The choir master will be disappointed if I waste my time on an adventure. You know, practice makes perfect."

"Yes, well, I am looking forward to hearing the finished version. Good day, my lady."

Two for two, Wally thought. *Not very good odds*. His friends were usually ready to do something fun, so he didn't understand why Aspen and Ivy didn't want to have fun today.

He continued on his way and ran across Billy Bear. Billy was the only boy out of three cubs and was always ready to get away from his annoying sisters. If anyone would be able to go on the adventure, it was Billy, or so Wally thought.

"Hi, Billy! Would you like to go on an adventure today?" asked Wally.

"Well, I can't. My mom said, I have to have a fishing lesson today. Maybe next time."

Wally was very disappointed that three of his friends didn't wanted to join him. Then he thought about the new kid on the block. Tommy Porcupine had just moved in not far from Wally's house, so Wally went in search of the new neighbor. When Wally found Tommy, he was standing in a small clearing.

Wally knew not to get too close to a porcupine, so he yelled, "Tommy!"

Tommy stopped and turned around.

"Oh, it's you, Wally. I'm glad you are here. Do you want to watch me do my target practice?"

"Not really. I am on an adventure, and I was wondering if you would like to come along. I could show you some cool places along the way. I'm a great tour guide."

"I'm sorry, Wally. I am practicing for the Junior Porcupine Olympics. My dad said, it should be a piece of cake for me to win this year. Last year I came in fifth."

"I'll see you another time then, Tommy. Good luck with your tournament."

Wally turned with a huff and headed slowly for the stream, but tears began to pool in the corner of his eyes so he started running. He didn't want the new kid to see him cry.

By the time Wally ran out of breath, his tears had dried up. Wally stopped to catch his breath and looked around. He had been to this part of the woods once with his mother, but he wasn't too sure if he should go any further because his parents told him this could be a dangerous place.

All of a sudden, a blue jay started dive bombing him. Running, he tried to duck each time the persistent bird came after him. Finally, he found a fallen tree that was hollow and crawled inside. He was grateful for the protection but knew he couldn't stay long if he wanted to continue his journey and return home before dark.

Wally took a chance and peeked out just as the bird began to screech.

"Hey, you're barking up the wrong tree!" Wally yelled before scooting back into the log. When the fuss was over, Wally climbed out and carefully looked around. Even though he knew he shouldn't go further by himself, he thought he would go just a little further.

The area had become a little rocky, and Wally heard water trickling nearby. He remembered what his mom had told him about watering holes, but he was so thirsty. Stopping for a drink of water, Wally enjoyed the taste of the fresh spring water.

The weather was warm, so Wally decided to take a quick sun bath. He found a comfortable spot and stretched out.

Not long after Wally closed his eyes he heard a frightening sound. He slowly looked over and saw a rattle snake. Wally slowly and quietly backed away. The snake began inhaling the scents around itself and suddenly Wally remembered the lessons his dad told him about rattle snakes. He tried to stay calm, but just when snake looked ready to strike a squirrel darted between them. Wally quickly climbed up the nearest tree and was surprised as the snake headed toward the squirrel, but the squirrel was too fast. Wally was grateful that the snake continued to crawl away. Now, he could continue his adventure.

Wally's stomach began to grumble. As he looked around, he noticed a clearing up ahead through the trees. His parents had warned him many times not to go out into open spaces to eat so he looked around and found a few tasty insects crawling nearby. Remembering that his mom had told him a thousand times that curiosity killed the cat, Wally almost began to go home, but he decided to go for broke and peeked through the trees anyway.

Wally saw a strange-looking thing in the middle of the meadow at the end of a road. It had four sides, which were made of smooth trees. He had never seen anything like this, but as he sat studying it, he realized this must be the thing his dad called a cabin. Cabins were places of great danger because that was where humans lived.

Wally sniffed the air and checked for signs of humans. He didn't smell, see, or hear anything that was alarming so he ran over to the cabin. He climbed on the ledge and looked around again for humans. None seemed to be around so he continued to check out the cabin. He saw a shiny round object sticking out and couldn't resist the urge to touch it. He stood on his tiptoes and began twisting the thing. Just when he heard a click, that part of the wall began to open.

As the hole opened more, a loud growl startled him. He jumped and spun around. There was a wolf at the edge of the tree line. His father always warned him to be more aware of his surroundings, but as usual, Wally got caught up in the moment. He knew he was in hot water now.

The wolf began approaching, and Wally began to shake. "Nice, doggy. I'm just going to turn around here and get out of your way. I hope you are all bark and no bite!"

The wolf started running toward Wally, so Wally hightailed it into the cabin and closed the opening. *That should do the trick*, he thought.

Wally leaned against the wall, thankful he was safe for now. He waited for the wolf to leave, but the wolf continued toward the cabin. Then all of a sudden, a howl was heard nearby and the beast's pack came running.

"Oh no, just what I need! You can't reach me so why don't you just give up and go home. Or better yet, go pick on someone your own size. I wouldn't taste very good anyway. My mom says I'm too tough for my own good."

Wally waited while the pack of wolves circled and circled the cabin. He finally sat down and tried to get comfortable.

Darkness began to fall and Wally was getting hungrier by the second. He noticed he hadn't heard any growling for a while, so he peeked through the window. He didn't see any wolves, so he checked the other window. Not seeing any wolves, he took a deep breath and relaxed grateful to have a roof over his head.

Now, Wally was super hungry. He saw some bags on one of the ledges so he climbed up. It took a few tries, but he got one bag opened and began eating the strange food. Then he sampled the other treats. Each one was unusual, and he wasn't sure if he liked them or not, but he couldn't stop eating. By the time he remembered what his parents told him about human food, it was too late. Instead of being hungry, now he had a stomachache. He felt terrible so he found a comfortable place to lie down.

27

Try as he might, Wally couldn't go to sleep. He kept thinking about all of the lessons his parents taught him and all of the rules he broke during his adventure. Wally didn't mean break all of the rules, but he kept going anyway. Now he was tired, scared, and his tummy ached like crazy; he realized how wrong he had been. It was then he was finally able to go to sleep.

Next thing he knew, light began to spill through the windows. He stretched and decided to skip breakfast so that he wouldn't waste time getting back home.

Wally was panting by the time he rounded the corner for home. He saw his mother sitting with her head in her paws, and he knew she was upset. He ran as fast as he could and threw his arms around her.

"Mom, don't worry. I'm home now," Wally said sorrowfully.

His mom looked up and began to cry harder.

Just then, Wally's dad walked up and began saying, "Wally Wilson Raccoon Jr., where have you been? Your mom and I have been worried sick! What have we told you about being home before dark? I can't—"

Wally's mom interrupted. "Let the boy answer your questions, Wally Sr."

"I know I was wrong," said Wally. "I know I should have obeyed the rules, but I got caught up in my adventure. When my stomach began to hurt from eating the human food, I realized that the rules you have taught me are meant to protect me. I am very sorry, and I won't do that again."

Wally Sr. said, "I am glad you learned your lesson. Next time you need to remember the rules before you do something. Now let's go eat.

About the Author

Chrys Wimer was born and raised in Central California where she currently resides. She attended various churches in the area where she was involved in many activities including the Awana Youth Organization. After graduating from The Master's College with a BA in psychology, she then received her teaching credential from CSU Fresno. Chrys has taught in various private schools where she taught at the elementary level and helped organized various events for K-12, including directing several vocal youth groups. She is currently a substitute teacher at the elementary level in CUSD.

Chrys enjoys spending time with family and friends. She has had the wonderful opportunity of traveling to Canada, England, France, Ireland, and Scotland as well as many states in the U.S. At the church she currently attends, Chrys serves in the worship team, choir, and the women's group. Chrys's hobbies include photography, baking, and crafting.

CPSIA information can be obtained
at www.ICGtesting.com
Printed in the USA
BVHW022025301118
534482BV00001B/6/P

9 781635 758498